WE BOTH READ®

Parent's Introduction

Whether your child is a beginning reader, a reluctant reader, or an eager reader, this book offers a fun and easy way to encourage and help your child in reading.

Developed with reading education specialists, *We Both Read* books invite you and your child to take turns reading aloud. You read the left-hand pages of the book, and your child reads the right-hand pages—which have been written at one of six early reading levels. The result is a wonderful new reading experience and faster reading development!

You may find it helpful to read the entire book aloud yourself the first time, then invite your child to participate the second time. As you read, try to make the story come alive by reading with expression. This will help to model good fluency. It will also be helpful to stop at various points to discuss what you are reading. This will help increase your child's understanding of what is being read.

In some books, a few challenging words are introduced in the parent's text, distinguished with **bold** lettering. Pointing out and discussing these words can help to build your child's reading vocabulary. If your child is a beginning reader, it may be helpful to run a finger under the text as each of you reads. Please also notice that a "talking parent" ☺ icon precedes the parent's text, and a "talking child" ☺ icon precedes the child's text.

If your child struggles with a word, you can encourage "sounding it out," but keep in mind that not all words can be sounded out. Your child might pick up clues about a word from the picture, other words in the sentence, or any rhyming patterns. If your child struggles with a word for more than five seconds, it is usually best to simply say the word.

Most of all, remember to praise your child's efforts and keep the reading fun. After you have finished the book, ask a few questions and discuss what you have read together. Rereading this book multiple times may also be helpful for your child.

Try to keep the tips above in mind as you read together, but don't worry about doing everything right. Simply sharing the enjoyment of reading together will increase your child's reading skills and help to start your child off on a lifetime of reading enjoyment!

The Mighty Little Lion Hunter
We Both Read® Book

For my daughter Kellie. You are my joy and inspiration.
—J. C.

For Bob Call, The Mighty Little Junk Hunter.
—B. S.

Text Copyright © 2000 by Treasure Bay, Inc.
Illustrations Copyright © 2000 by Bob Staake
All rights reserved

We Both Read® is a trademark of Treasure Bay, Inc.

Published by Treasure Bay, Inc.
P.O. Box 119
Novato, CA 94948 USA

Printed in Singapore

Library of Congress Number: 00 130172

Hardcover ISBN: 978-1-891327-21-6
Paperback ISBN: 978-1-891327-22-3

We Both Read® Books
Patent No. 5,957,693

Visit us online at:
www.webothread.com

PR-11-12

WE BOTH READ™

THE
MIGHTY LITTLE
LION HUNTER

By Jana Carson

Illustrated by Bob Staake

TREASURE BAY

This is a story about **Kibu**.
Kibu was a proud member of the Masai
tribe in East Africa.

One day, **Kibu**'s big brothers were going
off to **hunt** for lions. **Kibu** wanted to be a
mighty lion hunter too.

Kibu said,
"I want
to go.
I want
to **hunt**."

Kibu's brothers laughed at him.

"No," they said, "you are too small. Father **Lion** will gobble you up— snip snap!"

Kibu did not like being laughed at.

Kibu said, "I will get a **lion**. You will see."

Kibu told his mother he was going to hunt for a lion.

"Little lion hunters **need** food," Kibu's mother said as she handed him a basket filled with yams, peanuts, and sour milk.

Kibu took the basket and set off into the jungle. As he walked, he talked to himself.

Kibu said, "I will **need** help. Who will help me?"

Sister Rain was listening high in the sky. "Why will you need help?" she called down kindly to Kibu.

Kibu told **Rain** what he planned to do.

"Father Lion will gobble you up— snip snap!" said **Rain**.

"Will you help me, **Sister Rain**?" Kibu asked.

Sister Rain said, "What will you give to me?"

"I will give you my shield to protect you from Lightning when he throws his white spears to Earth," Kibu answered.

"I accept your gift," said Rain. "And when you need my help, I will give it."

Kibu continued his hunt for a lion. As he walked, he talked to himself.

Kibu said, "I will need help. Who will help me?"

Brother Elephant was watching through the trees. "Why will you need help?" he trumpeted to Kibu.

Kibu told **Elephant** what he planned to do.

"Father Lion will gobble you up—snip snap!" said **Elephant**.

"Will you help me, **Brother Elephant**?" Kibu asked.

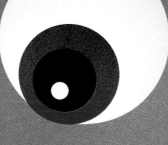 **Brother Elephant said, "What will you give to me?"**

⌾ "I will give you all the delicious peanuts from my basket," Kibu answered.

"I accept your gift," said Elephant. "And when you need my help, I will give it."

Elephant took Kibu to the river where Father Lion was often found. As Kibu stood on the river's edge, he talked to himself.

Kibu said,
"I need help.
Who will
help me?"

Mother Crocodile was swimming in the river. "Why will you need help?" she growled up to Kibu.

Kibu told **Crocodile** what he planned to do.

"Father Lion will gobble you up—snip snap!" said **Crocodile**.

"Will you help me, **Mother Crocodile**?" Kibu asked.

Mother Crocodile said, "What will you give to me?"

"I will give you my
gourd of sour milk
so that you may feed
your hungry babies,"
Kibu answered.

"I accept your gift," said
Crocodile. "And when you
need my help, I will give it."

Then Mother Crocodile
offered to help Kibu **find**
Father Lion.

Kibu said, "Yes! We will **find** a lion."

 It wasn't long before they did find Father Lion, resting beneath a tree.

"How do you **plan** to catch him?" asked Mother Crocodile.

Kibu told her that he was a mighty hunter.

Kibu said,
"I have a **plan**.
A good, good
plan!"

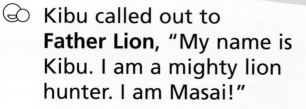 Kibu called out to **Father Lion**, "My name is Kibu. I am a mighty lion hunter. I am Masai!"

Father Lion looked at the little hunter and was very puzzled.

Father Lion said, "Why do you call me?

What do you want?"

"I want to have a contest with you," Kibu replied.

Now it was known in every village that all lions loved a good contest. And Father Lion was no different.

Father Lion said,
"Tell me more.
Tell me more."

"You will have three chances to eat me up," Kibu said. "If you win, your belly will be full."

"And if I **lose**?" said Father Lion.

Kibu said,
"If you **lose**,
I will win."

 Father Lion was losing his patience. "Tell me what will happen if I lose or I will eat you up right now!"

Kibu quickly pulled a rope from his basket and said, "If you lose, you must promise to come back with me to my village on the end of this rope!"

Father Lion said, "I will not lose. I will win!"

Father Lion promised to follow the rules of the contest, then jumped up quickly and pounced on little Kibu!

Kibu said, "Help me, Mother Crocodile! I need help!"

Mother Crocodile
raced in quickly
and snapped her
powerful jaws
on Father Lion's
tail.

"Y-E-E-OUCH!!"

Father Lion let go of Kibu with a yelp.
Kibu escaped and scrambled to the top
of a great, huge rock. But soon Father
Lion was after him again!

Kibu said,
"Help me,
Brother
Elephant!
I need help!"

Brother Elephant thundered in and lifted Kibu high into the air to gently place him on his back. Then Elephant carried Kibu back to his village.

Father Lion followed, roaring, "When I catch you, I will gobble you up!"

Kibu said, "Help me, Sister Rain! I need help!"

Rain appeared in the sky and pelted Father Lion with enormous raindrops. The drops fell so hard on Father Lion that he could not see. That is when Kibu ran up and placed the rope around Father Lion's neck.

Kibu said,
"I win, Father Lion!
I win!"

"You had three chances to eat me, and you have failed," said Kibu. "Now you must keep your promise!"

Kibu walked proudly into his village with the Father Lion on the end of his rope. Kibu's brothers saw this and were stunned!

Kibu said,
"Look at me,
brothers!
Look at
me!"

The elders of the village stopped what they were doing and stared. Kibu's mother and father were glowing with pride.

Everyone in the village shouted, "Look at the **mighty,** little lion **hunter!**"

Kibu said,
"I am a **hunter**!
A **mighty** lion hunter!"

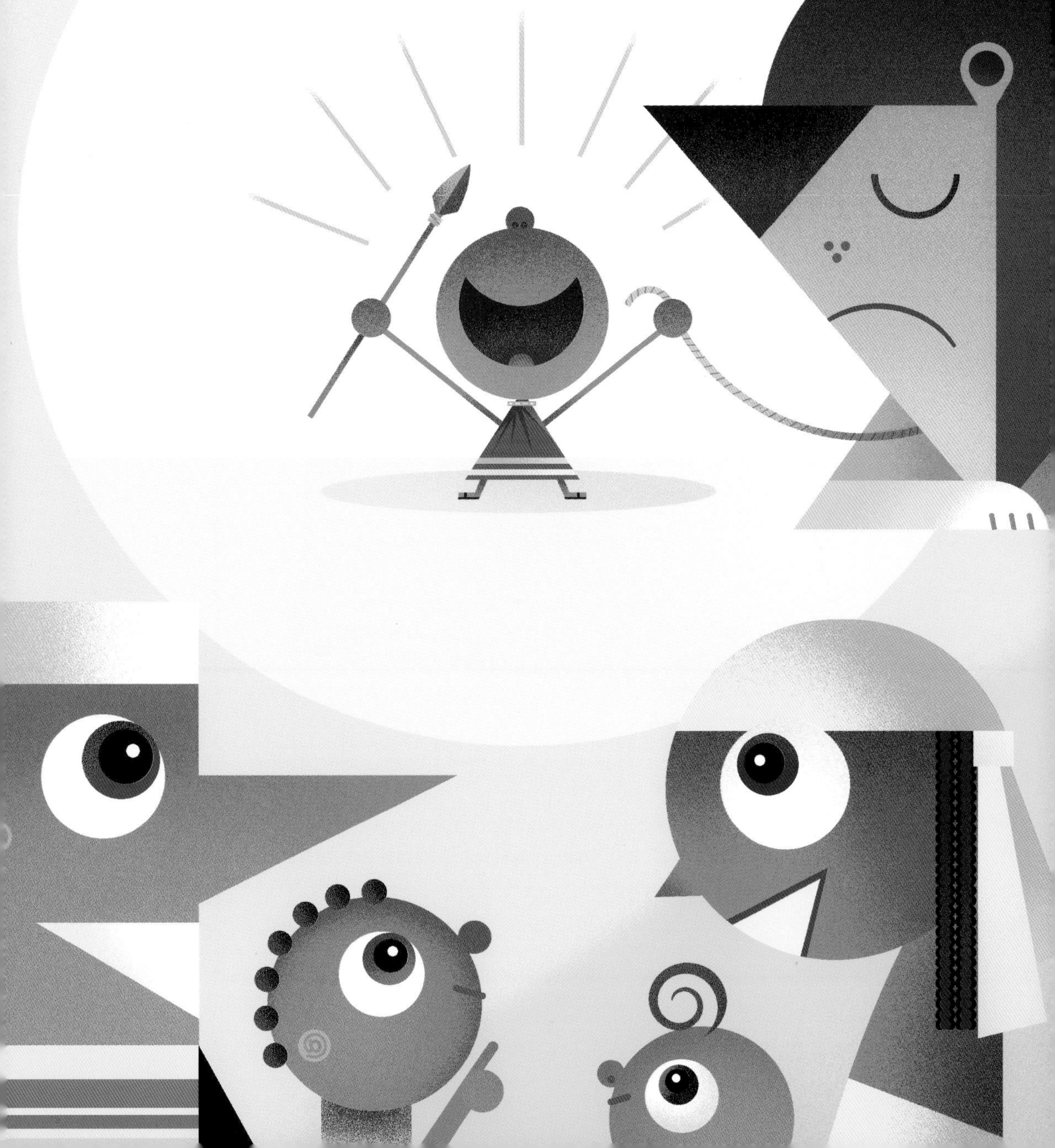

If you liked
***The Mighty Little Lion Hunter*, here are two other**
We Both Read™ **Books you are sure to enjoy!**

A very whimsical tale of a boy and his dog and their fantastic dreamland adventures. This delightful tale features fun and easy to read text for the very beginning reader, such as "pigs that dig", "fish on a dish", and a "dog on a frog."

To see all the We Both Read books that are available,
just go online to **www.webothread.com**

A very humorous updating of the classic story of
three little pigs and a very bad wolf. With short and
simple text for the very beginning reader, children
will be delighted to participate in reading aloud this
wonderful story.